Eva's Big Sleepover

Read more OWL DIARIES books!
1
OWL DIARIES
Eva's Treetop Festival
2
OWL DIARIES
Eva Sees a Ghost
3
OWL DIARIES
A Woodland Wedding
4
OWL DIARIES
Eva and the New Owl
5
OWL DIARIES
Warm Hearts Day
6
OWL DIARIES
Baxter Is Missing
7
OWL DIARIES
The Wildwood Bakery
8
OWL DIARIES
Eva and the Lost Pony
9
OWL DIARIES
Eva's Big Sleepover
10
OWL DIARIES
Eva and Baby Mo
Rebecca Elliott
SCHOLASTIC

OWL DIARIES

Eva's Big Sleepover

Rebecca
Elliott

BRANCHES™
SCHOLASTIC INC.

For the Peacock family,
my flaptastic feathery friends who
are always up for a party.—R.E.

Library of Congress Cataloging-in-Publication Data
Names: Elliott, Rebecca, author. | Elliott, Rebecca. Owl diaries ; 9.
Title: Eva's big sleepover / by Rebecca Elliott.
Description: First edition. | New York, NY : Branches/Scholastic Inc., 2018. | Series: Owl diaries ; 9 | Summary: Eva is planning a big sleepover for her "hatchday" celebration, but one of her friends, Sue, does not seem to want to attend—so Eva must find out what is bothering Sue, and help her get over her first-sleepover jitters.
Identifiers: LCCN 2018002079 | ISBN 9781338163063 (pbk) | ISBN 9781338163070 (hardcover)
Subjects: LCSH: Owls—Juvenile fiction. | Birthday parties—Juvenile fiction. | Sleepovers—Juvenile fiction. | Diaries—Juvenile fiction. | Friendship—Juvenile fiction. | CYAC: Owls—Fiction. | Birthdays—Fiction. | Parties—Fiction. | Sleepovers—Fiction. | Friendship—Fiction. | Diaries—Fiction.
Classification: LCC PZ7.E45812 Eu 2018 | DDC [Fic]—dc23 LC record available at https://lccn.loc.gov/2018002079

10 9 8 7 6 5 4 3 2 18 19 20 21 22

Printed in China 38
First edition, September 2018

Edited by Katie Carella
Book design by Marissa Asuncion

Table of Contents

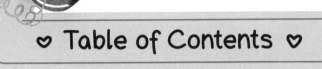

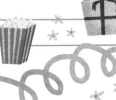

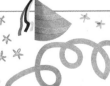

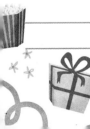

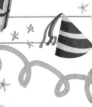

11
Woodpine Avenue

1

The Birthday Owl

Sunday

Hello lovely Diary,

It's me again: the one, the only . . . Eva Wingdale!

This week is going to be **SWOOPER-DUPER**! Do you want to know why? Next Saturday is my birthday!! (We owls also call this our **HATCHDAY**!)

I love:

Getting messy
when I make stuff

The word pebble

Playing cards
with my family

PRESENTS!

Really starry nights

Getting mail

Mom's wild-berry lemonade

Making friends laugh

I DO NOT love:

The word slug

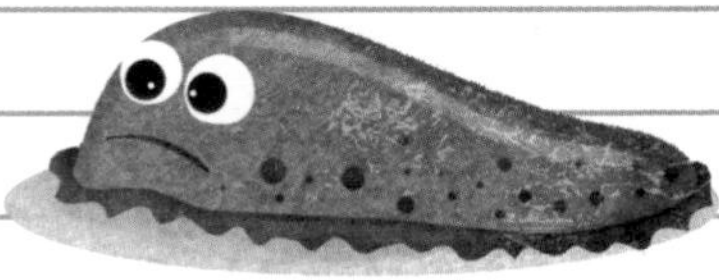

When my favorite clothes don't fit anymore

Baby Mo's gross eating habits

Loud thunder

Mom's roast leaf sandwich

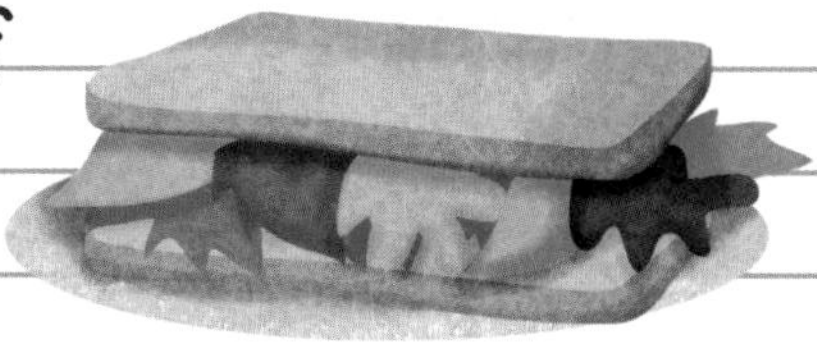

Feeling sick

When my book whacks me in the face (because I fall asleep when I'm reading!)

Making friends feel sad

My family is the best!

Here is a picture of me on my first birthday!

This is my baby brother, Mo, when he first hatched!

And here's the present my family gave me on my fifth birthday: my **OWLDORABLE** pet bat, BAXTER!

I love being an owl. Owls are the best!

We're asleep when the sun is out.

We're awake when the moon is out.

We come in all different shapes and sizes. The smallest owl is called an elf owl!

Owls can fly for miles before our wings get tired!

This is where I live.

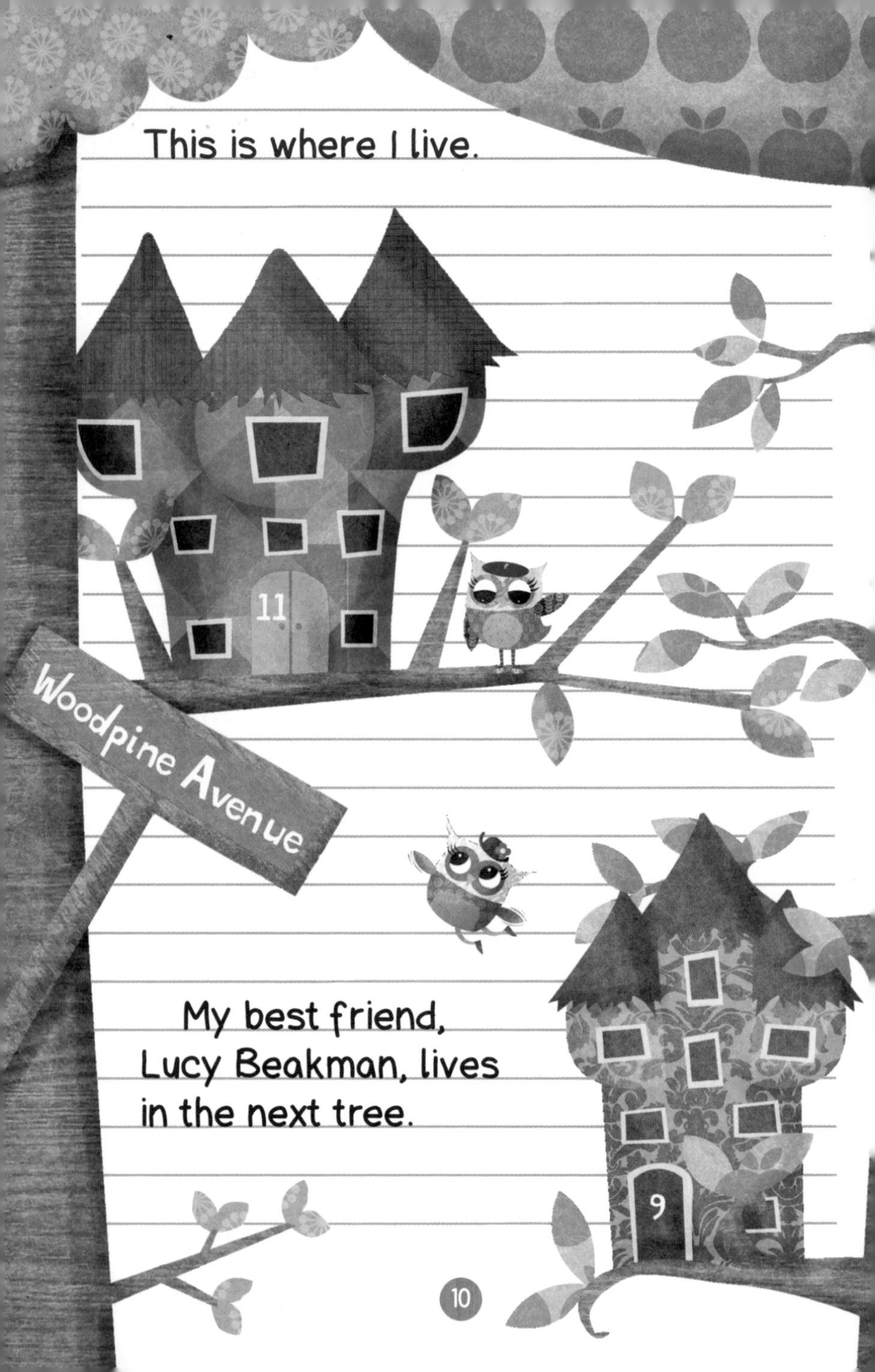

My best friend, Lucy Beakman, lives in the next tree.

This is my school.

Here's a photo of my class:

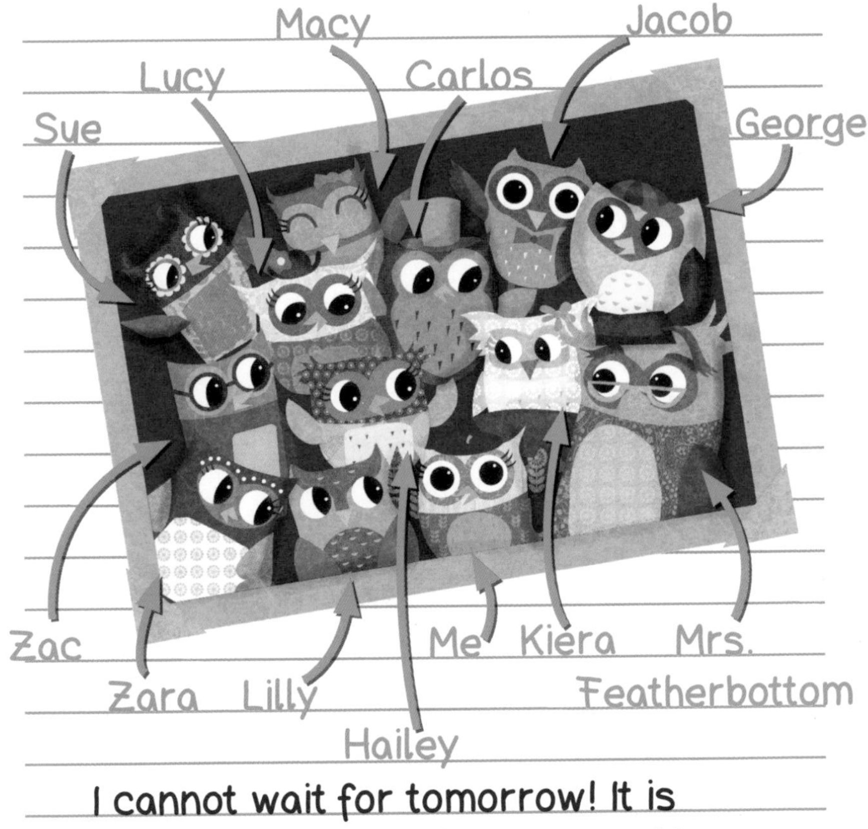

I cannot wait for tomorrow! It is show-and-tell day! (I have something **EGG-CELLENT** to show!) But it's bedtime. Good day, Diary!

2

♡ Party Plans ♡

Monday

We were all excited.

Quiet down, class!
It's show-and-tell time!

My classmates each shared something really **FLAPERRIFIC**.

Zara's photo diary

George's robot sheep model

Lilly's new book

Lucy's acorn animals

Carlos's magic trick

Zac's balloon rocket

Kiera's pinecone collection

Macy's beetle brownies

Jacob's new song

Hailey's fossil

Sue told the class about how she and her mom made a scarf together.

Sue's scarf

Wow, Sue! Your scarf is so pretty!
It looks owlmazing on me. Doesn't it?

Then it was my turn. I opened up the box I'd been hiding behind my back . . .

Everyone loved my show-and-tell.

But then Sue said something mean.

That looks like a BIG shell, Eva. You must have been a REALLY BIG chick!

My cheeks went a little red. I kept talking to change the subject.

I brought in this shell because it's actually my hatchday on Saturday.

That's wonderful, Eva. Happy early birthday!
Thank you! You're all invited to my party!
Yay!

At lunch, Lucy, Hailey, and I talked about my party plans.

I LOVE party planning!
Will your party be a sleepover party?
Oooh! I love that idea! I'll ask my mom.
That way, you can keep the fun going all day!

As soon as I got home, I talked to my mom.

A sleepover party is a great idea!
Wow! Thank you, Mom! It'll be WING-TASTIC!

But then I thought of something.

Mom asked me what was wrong.

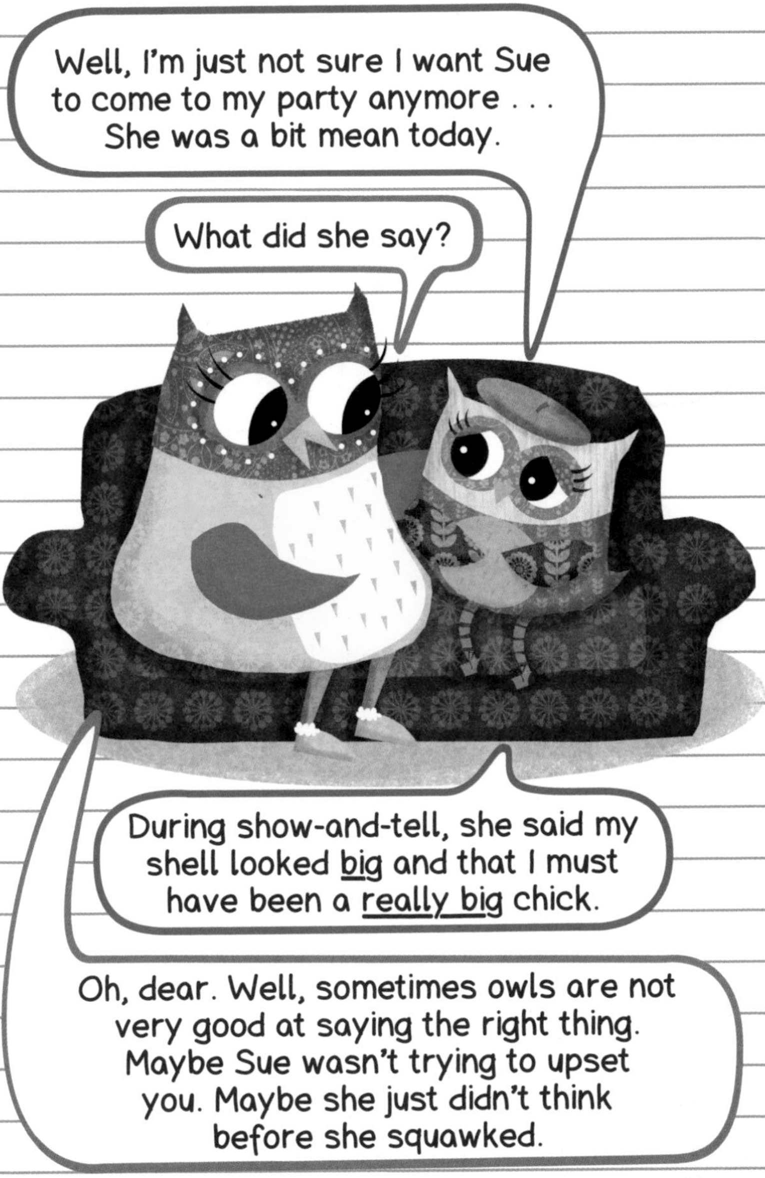
Well, I'm just not sure I want Sue to come to my party anymore . . . She was a bit mean today.
What did she say?
During show-and-tell, she said my shell looked big and that I must have been a really big chick.
Oh, dear. Well, sometimes owls are not very good at saying the right thing. Maybe Sue wasn't trying to upset you. Maybe she just didn't think before she squawked.

I guess so. But I'm still worried, Mom. Sue really ruffles my feathers. What if she ruins my special night?
If you don't invite her, then you'll be the mean one. And I know you don't want that.
No . . .
So invite her, Eva. It'll be fine. You'll have a great time. I'm sure of it.
Okay. Thanks, Mom.

My party is going to be **OWLSOME**! (At least it will be if Sue can be nice to me for a whole day!)

I made sleepover invitations for everyone in my class.

What do you think, Diary?

Now I'm going to dream about the best party ever!

3

♡ Keep Your Beak Shut! ♡

Tuesday

On the way to school, I told Lucy the good news.

Before class, I flew around giving out my brand-new sleepover party invitations.

Hailey was so excited she said we should start a party-planning club.

That's a great idea! I'll need help planning my BIG sleepover party.
We'll be the Sleepover Squad! I'll gather our best party-planning friends. We'll have the first club meeting tomorrow at lunch.
Yippee!

Then it was time to invite Sue . . .

I felt a little nervous as I flew over to her.

Is something wrong, Eva?
I just sort of wish I didn't have to invite Sue. I'm worried she'll be mean to me.

But I must have said that a bit too loudly, because Lucy suddenly said –

Sue was standing right behind us! EEEEEK! I grabbed Lucy's wing and pulled her aside.

Oh no! Do you think Sue heard what I said?!
I don't know. Maybe. Maybe not. Either way, you need to invite her NOW before she hears about your sleepover party from someone else.
You're right. Okay, okay!

I flew over to Sue. My wings were shaking, but I tried to sound normal.

Hello, Sue! How are you on . . . this . . . lovely Tuesday?
Fine.
Great! So, you know I'm having my birthday party on Saturday. Well, now it's a sleepover party! Can you come?
Hmm. No. I think I'll be busy then.

Sue flew to her seat.

ARGHHHH!!!

I feel AWFUL! Sue <u>must have</u> heard what I said to Lucy! I hate to think that I hurt her feelings.

I kept trying to talk to Sue for the rest of the night. But she always flew away. How can I say I'm sorry if she won't listen to me?

Oh, Diary, I never should have said anything about not wanting to invite Sue.

Mom was right — that makes me the mean one! I guess if you're mean about the meany, that makes you the meany.

4

♡ Sleepover Squad ♡

Wednesday

I wanted to talk to Sue tonight. But Hailey called the first Sleepover Squad meeting at lunch. So I couldn't get away.

I want to hear everyone's sleepover ideas!
Ice cream buffet!
Photo booth!
Decorate pillows!
Play pin-the-beak-on-the-owl!
Watch a movie!

There were so many **FLAP-TASTIC** ideas! I added one, too: We could all sleep in tents in my room!

Then I wrote a to-do list.

1. Make a sign for the ice cream buffet
2. Get the photo booth ready
3. Set up a pillowcase crafting corner
4. Paint a big owl for the pin-the-beak-on-the-owl game
5. Cook popcorn for the movie
6. Put up and decorate tents

During recess, everyone was playing **WINGBALL**. I saw Sue sitting on her own, so I flew up to her.

Then she flew off. Again.

Lucy saw what happened. She flew over to me.

Sue must have heard what you said.
I know. She must think I don't want her at the sleepover. That's why she said she can't come. I just feel so bad about it. But how can I make it right if she won't talk to me?

What if we fly to her tree house after school?
That's a great idea! She'll have to listen then. I can say sorry and tell her I really do want her at my sleepover.

After school, Lucy and I flew to Sue's house.

Sue opened the door. My voice was squeaky, but I knew I had to speak up and say the right thing.

Hello, Sue. I just . . . I wanted to say I'm so sorry for what I said at school.

I thought Sue would get mad or slam the door. But she just looked at me strangely.

What? What did you say at school?
Sue hadn't heard me after all!
Oh, nothing! I didn't say anything. Did you say anything, Lucy?
No, nothing at all.
So . . . why are you here?
Um . . .

Just then, Sue's mom flew home.

Sue's mom flew inside.

Your mom said you can come! That's great, Sue!
No . . . Look, I'm sorry, Eva. I'll come to your party until my mom picks me up. But I can't sleep over.

Then she slammed the door right in our beaks!

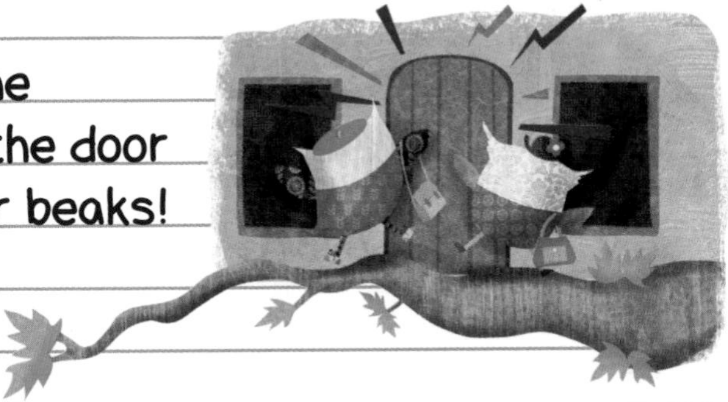

Well, thank goodness Sue didn't hear what you said in class.
I know! I'll never say anything bad about anyone ever again.
But I'm confused. If Sue is not upset about what you said, and if she's not busy with her mom, then why won't she sleep over?
I don't know. It's a mystery!

5

The Mystery of Sue

Thursday

I called an emergency Sleepover Squad meeting. I told everyone how Sue said she can't sleep over, but how it seemed like she could sleep over if she really wanted to.

It's too bad Sue is not staying over.

This would be the first time we'll all have a sleepover together.
It won't feel right without her.
We must do something about it — Operation Sue!
No owl left behind!

We decided that if Sue doesn't want to sleep over, then that must mean one of two things:

1. Sue doesn't like sleepovers, or
2. Sue doesn't like me.

So we came up with a secret plan to find out the truth!

First, George talked to Sue.

So now we know she likes sleepovers!

Next, Hailey talked to Sue.
Hey, Sue. I'm writing an article for the class newspaper. It's about everyone's best qualities. What should I write about Eva?
That's easy! Eva is kind, funny, and creative.

Sue said such nice things about me.

Sue flew past. I took the chance to ask her again – in front of everyone.

Hey, Sue! Please stay for my sleepover. Everyone wants you to. Right, everyone?
Yeah!
It'll be fun!
Everyone else will be there!

Sue went really red in the face. And she squawked at me!

I JUST DON'T WANT TO COME TO YOUR SILLY SLEEPOVER!! OKAY?!

Then Sue flew to class.

We all flew inside, too.

I felt a bit upset. I'd never been squawked at before.

Don't worry, Eva. Your sleepover party is going to be HOOTERRIFIC with or without Sue.
Thanks, Lucy. I guess you're right. And we still have so much to do for the party!

After school, the Sleepover Squad met at my tree house.

George and Hailey made the sign for the ice cream buffet.

Zara and Zac got the photo booth ready.

Lucy and I set up the pillowcase crafting corner.

Then we all had a pillow fight. It was such a **HOOT**!

I can't wait for Saturday! I just wish I knew why Sue won't sleep over, and why she got so upset tonight.

It's sort of funny how I didn't want Sue to come to my sleepover because I thought she might ruin it, but now I'm worried that Sue NOT being there might ruin it more! I just wish everyone could be together.

6

How to Make a Sleepover

Friday

Sue didn't really talk to anyone at school. Sometimes she is quiet when she's in a mean mood. But tonight, Sue seemed kind of sad. How can I help if she won't talk to me?

After school, the Sleepover Squad came over again. We kept working on our to-do list.

1. Make a sign for the ice cream buffet
2. Get the photo booth ready
3. Set up a pillowcase crafting corner
4. Paint a big owl for the pin-the-beak-on-the-owl game
5. Cook popcorn for the movie
6. Put up and decorate tents

Lucy and Zac painted the owl for the pin-the-beak-on-the-owl game.

Hailey and I cooked the movie popcorn. We even made little boxes to put it in!

Zara and George put up the tents and painted them.

We kept decorating . . .

Finally, everything was ready for my party.

Photo Booth
PIN THE BEAK ON THE OWL!
It looks OWLMAZING!
I can't wait until tomorrow!

7

♡ Happy Hatchday! ♡

Saturday

HAPPY **HATCHDAY** TO ME!

It has been a totally **OWLSOME** birthday! My party was great! We danced and played games. (And I tried not to think about how Sue was going to leave early.)

Here's a list of some of my presents:

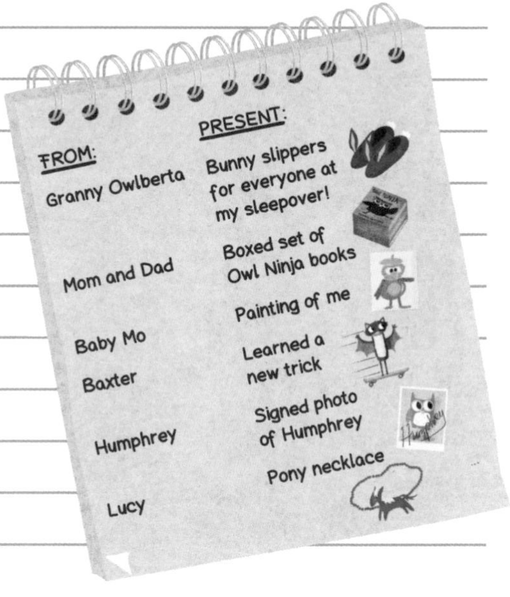
FROM:
PRESENT:
Granny Owlberta
Bunny slippers for everyone at my sleepover!
Mom and Dad
Boxed set of Owl Ninja books
Painting of me
Baby Mo
Learned a new trick
Baxter
Signed photo of Humphrey
Humphrey
Pony necklace
Lucy

Then Carlos gave me a present that changed <u>everything</u>: a truth-or-dare card game. In the game, you are asked a question. If you don't answer it, you have to do a silly dare.

We started playing the game. At first, it was really fun!

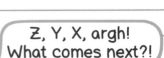

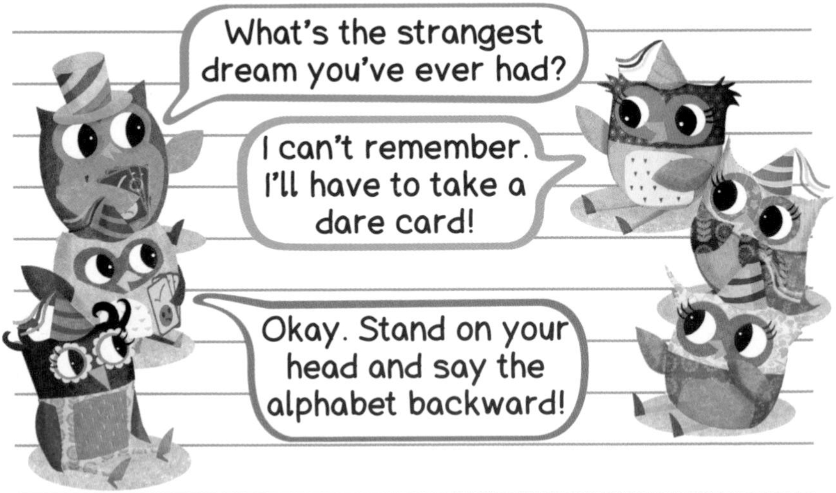
What's the strangest dream you've ever had?
I can't remember. I'll have to take a dare card!
Okay. Stand on your head and say the alphabet backward!

Z, Y, X, argh! What comes next?!

Everyone laughed.

Next it was my turn.

Name something you're scared of.
Hmmm . . . So I know this sounds silly, but I have my first OWLADONTIST appointment next week. And I'm really scared.
Eva, that is silly. There is nothing scary about the OWLADONTIST!
I know. It's just that I've never been before.

Suddenly, I had a BIG idea!

That's it!
That's what?
Oh . . . nothing!

I pulled Lucy into the kitchen.

Lucy, I think I know why Sue doesn't want to sleep over.
Really? Why?
The same reason I'm scared of going to the OWLADONTIST. She's never been before!
Ooooh! That makes sense! So what should we do?
I'm going to try talking with her about it. Wish me luck!

I flew over to Sue.

Hey, Sue. I'm sorry if I was a bit pushy before – about you sleeping over tonight.
That's okay. I'm sorry I squawked at you.
That's okay. But, um, I was wondering if . . . maybe you haven't been to a sleepover before?

I thought she was going to get mad at me for asking. But then –

Sue looked at the floor.

You're right. I haven't been to a sleepover before because, well, I've just never been invited before. I really do want to stay over, but the truth is I'm a bit scared.

Just like I'm scared about the OWLADONTIST! But like you said, it's not scary really. I'm just scared because it's new and I've never been before. I think if you stay for my sleepover, you'll be having too much fun to be scared!

Do you really think so?

I do. It will definitely be more fun than the OWLADONTIST!

Sue laughed.

Everyone else flew over.
I was really scared on my first sleepover!
Me too!
And me!

Just then, Sue's mom came to take her home. Sue flew over to her.

Mom, I was thinking . . .
I might like to sleep over now.
Darling, I hoped you might change your mind. I brought your pajamas just in case!

Everyone cheered.

8

Sleepover Success!

Sunday

The sleepover last night was **FLAPPY-FABULOUS**!

We ate ice cream.

We took pictures in the photo booth.

We had a HUGE pillow fight where we ended up in a pillow mountain!

We played pin-the-beak-on-the-owl.

We watched the movie and ate popcorn.

Then Sue had a great idea for a new activity: a pajama fashion show!

While everyone was getting ready, Sue flew over to me.

Thanks for getting me to stay, Eva. You were right. Sleepovers are SUPER!
You're welcome, Sue! I'm glad you're having fun. My hatchday wouldn't be the same without you.
I almost forgot! Here's your present.

It was Sue's HOOTIFUL scarf!
I could tell how much you liked it during show-and-tell. Happy birthday, Eva!
Really? This is for me? Thanks, Sue!
Eva's Pajama Fashion Show

HAPPY BIRTHDAY, EVA!

We stayed up partying into the day! So we've only just settled into our tents. This has been THE BEST BIRTHDAY!

And I have to say it was only <u>this</u> **FLAP-TASTIC** because EVERYONE was here to celebrate it with me.

I guess we all get scared and need a little help and understanding sometimes. Even Sue! See you next time, Diary!

Rebecca Elliott was a lot like Eva when she was younger: She loved making things and hanging out with her best friends. Now that Rebecca is older, not much has changed — except that her best friends are her husband, Matthew, and their children. She still loves making things, like stories, cakes, music, and paintings. But as much as she and Eva have in common, Rebecca cannot fly or turn her head all the way around. No matter how hard she tries.

Rebecca is the author of JUST BECAUSE and MR. SUPER POOPY PANTS. OWL DIARIES is her first early chapter book series.

OWL DIARIES

How much do you know about Eva's Big Sleepover?

I am the smallest type of owl in the world. What am I called? Reread Chapter 1.

On page 32, Eva apologizes to Sue for saying something mean at school. Have you ever accidentally hurt a friend's feelings? How did you say sorry?

I am a good friend to Eva. What are <u>two</u> things I do to help Eva in this book? Reread Chapters 3-5 for examples.

What's the <u>real</u> reason I don't want to sleep over at Eva's party?

The Sleepover Squad organizes fun activities for Eva's sleepover, like a pillowcase crafting corner and an ice cream buffet. Imagine <u>your</u> dream sleepover. What activities and games would you plan? Draw a picture of your sleepover!

scholastic.com/branches